*. . . for parents and teachers*

Sibling rivalry! How the term strikes fear and anxiety in the hearts of parents. We want brothers to love each other; we wish for sisters to be companions. Immature outbursts of anger alarm us, and seem to call for quick intervention and preaching about the moral goal of brotherly love. A child's cry of "I hate you" seems to forecast a lifelong pattern of sibling alienation.

In this sensitive and simple story, the author strikes a chord of memory in all who have ever had a sib. The hero seems full of hate and jealousy, but the story carefully uncovers him as an imposter who both loves and misses his adversary. The recognition of this ambivalence and its resolution is at the heart of developmental growth.

*Will I Ever Be Older?* reminds us that there are always two sides to every emotional story, as David and Steven are shown to be more alike than unalike in their feelings. This story will stimulate many discussions, as it provides a useful reminder to both parent and child of the universal nature of the sibling experience.

LaMar M. Fox, M.D.
Vice President and Executive
   Director, Child Guidance Clinic
Children's Hospital
   and Health Center
San Diego, California

Eva Grant is the author of six books and
over 100 stories and articles for children.
She lives in New Jersey.

Library of Congress Number: 80-24782

7  8  9  10  11  12      95  94  93  92  91

**Library of Congress Cataloging in Publication Data**

Grant, Eva.
  Will I ever be older?

  SUMMARY: A younger brother comes to recognize that
though he often resents his older brother, his brother
has sibling difficulties, too.
  (1. Sibling rivalry — Fiction) I. Lexa, Susan.
II. Title.
PZ7.G76674Wi    (Fic.)    80-24782
ISBN 0-8172-1363-5 lib. bdg.

# WILL
# I EVER BE
# OLDER?

by *Eva Grant*

*illustrated by Susan Lexa*

introduction by LaMar M. Fox, M.D.

**RAINTREE
STECK-VAUGHN
L I B R A R Y**
A Division of Steck-Vaughn Company

Steven was born before I was. He's so lucky.

Now he's ten. I'm seven. When he's eleven, I'll be eight. Even when he's thirty-three, I'll only be thirty.

I'll never catch up to him.

I hardly ever get new clothes.

When Steven gets new shirts, I get his old ones. When he gets new jeans, I get his old jeans.

Sometimes his old jeans have a patch on them. I *hate* wearing jeans with patches.

I get Steven's old soccer shoes. And his old soccer ball.

I get his old roller skates — without a skate key.

I even get his old teachers.

Sometimes Ms. Hardy says, "David, why can't you be more like your brother? Steven was hardly ever late to school."

Or, "Steven would never talk to me like that."

Or, "Steven always had his homework done. Why don't you?"

Sometimes people don't even seem to remember my name.

Once in a while Grandma calls me Steven.

"I'm *David*," I tell her.

But she forgets. "Come here, Steven," she says.

It's things like that that make me sometimes wish there *were* no Steven.

Last week, Mom and I drove over to pick Steven up after his soccer practice. He wasn't waiting for us where he should have been.

Mom was worried, but I wasn't.

"Maybe we'll never find him," I said. "And then I'll get to be the oldest."

Mom gave me a funny look.

Then I asked, "Mom, do you think I will ever be older than Steven?" I knew it was kind of a silly question, but it's something I always wonder about.

"No," Mom said gently. "But maybe being the oldest isn't always so great."

"What do you mean?"

"When Steven was born," Mom said, "Dad and I didn't know much about taking care of babies. We sort of practiced on Steven, and we were really nervous. But when you came along, you were lots of fun."

"It's no fun for me," I said. "I have to go to bed before he does. He gets to watch all the good TV programs. He's always the lucky one."

"When Steven was your age," Mom said, "he had to go to bed much earlier than you do now."

"I don't believe Steven ever *was* my age," I grumbled.

Mom sighed and looked out the window.

I could tell Mom was getting more
worried about Steven, so I tried to think of
something to cheer her up.

*I* wasn't worried, but I was getting tired
of sitting around. So I said, "I'll go and
see if I can find Steven in the locker
room."

"Thank you, David," Mom said.

As I ran up the walk, I thought about
Steven and the soccer team. You had to be
eight years old to join the team. It was
just one more thing I was too young to do.

Then I saw Steven running down the walk toward me.

"Where's Mom?" he shouted. "I can't wait to tell her the news!"

Without waiting for me to answer, he ran right past me, almost knocking me over.

I followed Steven as he took my place on the bench.

"Mom," said Steven, "I've been asked to go to a soccer clinic!"

"What's a clinic?" I asked.

Steven didn't even look at me. He just kept talking to Mom. "It's two whole days of doing nothing but playing soccer," he said. "A famous soccer player is going to give us tips on playing better soccer. Can I go, Mom? Please?"

Mom looked at me. "When is the clinic, and who can go?" she asked.

"It's this weekend," said Steven. "And it's only for team members."

Of course, Steven got to go to the soccer clinic.

And I got to spend all weekend by myself.

I kicked around Steven's old soccer ball for a while. But there was no one to kick it back to me.

I tried out Steven's old roller skates. But only Steven knows how to get them to fit right.

I got to stay up late Saturday to watch a TV program. It was one of Steven's favorite shows, but he wasn't there to laugh at it with me.

Finally Steven came home, full of funny stories about the clinic. He kept all of us laughing for a long time — even me. I was surprised at how nice it felt to have Steven back.

After we had gone to bed and all the lights were turned off, I told him about the old soccer ball and the roller skates, and about the old jeans and shirts. I even told him about Ms. Hardy and Grandma.

I told him I didn't *really* mind.

Steven was just about asleep, but then he opened his eyes. "Sometimes Grandma calls me David," he said.